W9-BFC-612

Black and White Rabbit's ABC

Alan Baker

KINGFISHER
NEW YORK

ALEXANDRIA LIBRARY
ALEXANDRIA, VA 22304

KINGFISHER
LONDON & NEW YORK

Copyright © Alan Baker 1994
Published in the United States by Kingfisher,
175 Fifth Ave., New York, NY 10010
Kingfisher is an imprint of Macmillan Children's Books, London.
All rights reserved.

Distributed in the U.S. by Macmillan,
175 Fifth Ave., New York, NY 10010
Distributed in Canada by H.B. Fenn and Company Ltd.,
34 Nixon Road, Bolton, Ontario L7E 1W2

LIBRARY OF CONGRESS CATALOGING-IN-PUBLICATION DATA
Baker, Alan.
Black and White Rabbit's ABC/Alan Baker.—1st American ed.
p. cm.— (Little rabbit books)
Summary: The story of a rabbit's exhausting efforts to
paint a picture presents the letters of the alphabet.
[1. Alphabet. 2. Painting—Fiction. 3. Rabbits—Fiction.]
I. Title. II. Series: Baker, Alan. Little rabbit books.
PZ7.B1688B1 1994
[E]—dc20 93-29760 CIP AC

ISBN: 978-0-7534-5253-0

For more information, please visit
www.kingfisherpublications.com

Printed in Singapore
15 14 13 12 11

Aa

A is for apple.

Bb

B is for box,
where Rabbit
puts the apple.

Cc

C is for crayon,
held in Rabbit's paw.

Dd

D is for drawing.

Ee

E is for easel,
to rest Rabbit's
drawing on.

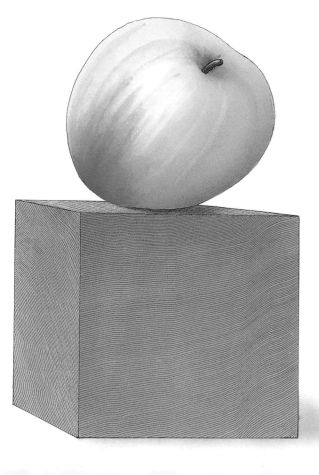

Ff

F is for falling
as the apple
topples over.

Gg

G is for glue,
icky-sticky
glue.

Hh

H is for hopping,
with a sticky paw.

Ii

I is for ink bottle,
right in Rabbit's way.

Jj

J is for jumping,
but not high enough!

Kk

K is for
kicking
it over.
Whoops!

Ll

L is for leaking
all over the floor.

Mm

M is the mess,
soon mopped up.

INK

Nn

N is for nose,
covered in ink.

Oo

O is for
opening
a new jar
of paint.

Pp

P is for the
paint,

a bright
apple
green.

Qq

Q is for quick! Paint in the picture.

Rr

R is for runny, the paint's not thick enough.

Ss

S is for spilling as paint drips off the brush.

Tt

T is for
turning.

Uu

U is for
upside down.

Vv

V is for very good.
Rabbit's painting
is done.

W w

W is for water
to wash
the brushes.

Xx

X is for the kisses
that Rabbit
draws on his
painting.

Yy

Y is for yawning. What a hard day's work!

Zz

Z is for zzzzzzzzz.
Rabbit's fast asleep.

RECEIVED

JUL 27 2010

BY:_____